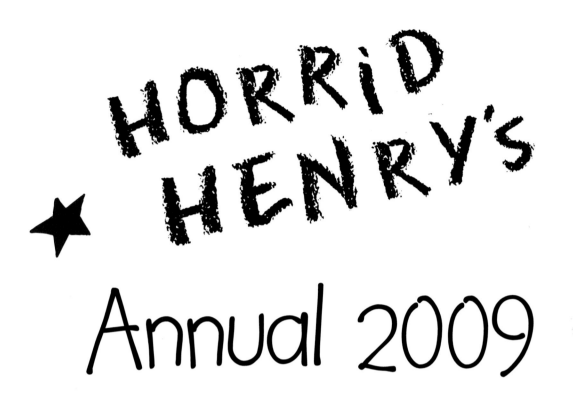

Annual 2009

HORRID HENRY'S
Annual 2009

Francesca Simon

Illustrated by Tony Ross

Orion
Children's Books

This edition produced for The Book People Ltd.
Hall Wood Avenue,
Haydock, St. Helens WA11 9UL

First published in Great Britain in 2008
by Orion Children's Books
a division of the Orion Publishing Group Ltd
Orion House
5 Upper Saint Martin's Lane
London WC2H 9EA

1 3 5 7 9 10 8 6 4 2

The Orion Publishing Group's policy is to use papers that are natural, renewable and
recyclable products and made from wood grown in sustainable forests. The logging
and manufacturing processes are expected to conform to the environmental
regulations of the country of origin.

ISBN 978 1 4072 1494 8

A catalogue record for this book is available from the British Library

Printed and bound in Italy by Rotolito Lombarda

www.orionbooks.co.uk
www.horridhenry.co.uk

Contents

Hello Everyone,

Welcome to my brilliant fantastic annual. I'm on nearly every page – LOADS more than poopy pants Peter. Nah nah ne nah nah!

Mum and Dad nagged me to make some New Year's Resolutions – stupid stuff like keeping my room tidy or eating bleuch . . . vegetables. Yuck! No way!

Here are My New Year's Resolutions:

To be crowned King Henry the Horrible – watch out, Peter!

To defeat my evil enemies and drop them into vats of glop.

To make loads of money and spend it all on toys and sweets for ME – he he!

It's going to be my best year ever!

Henry

Can you help me find the ten gold gizmos hidden throughout the book?

King Henry the Horrible's Royal Rules

This is what I'll look like when I'm crowned King of the World, the Universe and everywhere. I'll make loads of rules and everyone will have to obey me . . . or else! That slimy toad Peter will be sorry he ever got me into trouble.

KING HENRY'S ROYAL RULES

The King is allowed to:
- Eat as many sweets as he likes
- Stay up as late as he wants
- Watch TV all day and all night
- Demand £1,000 pocket money a week

TOP RULE
Anyone who dares to say no to King Henry, will have to do chores for ever!

VERY IMPORTANT RULE – MUST BE OBEYED
Smelly little brothers must go to their rooms and stay there for a whole year with NO TV. Bye bye Peter pants face – see you next year!

VERY IMPORTANT RULE NUMBER 2
Anyone named Margaret will give all their toys to King Henry.

RULES FOR PARENTS

- Any parent who makes their children go on hikes will be dumped barefoot in a scorpion-infested desert
- Anyone who says the word 'homework' will get thrown to the crocodiles
- Any parent who so much as whispers the word 'chores' will get catapulted over the battlements into a moat full of piranhas

SCHOOL RULES

- Parents have to go to school, instead of children
- On Sports' Day the teachers have to run all the races, and King Henry will present the winners with loads of homework
- Only sweets are allowed for school dinners. Vegetables are forbidden

If you were King, what would your most important rules be?

MY ROYAL RULES

_____

_____

_____

_____

_____

_____

_____

Horrid Henry's Evil Enemies

Some of Horrid Henry's most evil enemies are his family. Henry has written about their wicked ways around the family photo, but can you work out who did what?

B: Vomited all over me. Aaaggghhh!

E: Lost a tooth before me and got money from the tooth fairy, and I got nothing.

J: Called me Henrietta and sent me pink lacy knickers for my birthday.

I: Forced me to go to dancing classes at Miss Impatience Tutu's Dance Studio. I soon put a stop to that – ha ha!

DAD   MUM

GRANDMA

STUCK-UP STEVI

PERFECT PETER

Draw arrows from the picture to the text to show who did what.

Grandma   ___   Dad   ___

Mum   ___   Great-Aunt Greta   ___

Rich Aunt Ruby ___   Perfect Peter   ___

Stuck-up Steve ___   Vomiting Vera   ___

Pimply Paul   ___   Prissy Polly   ___

D: Invited me to sta made me play with

C: Forced me to be a page-boy at her wedding and wear stupid clothes.

G: Married Prissy Polly and called me a brat.

F: Tried to scare me at night when I stayed at his house. Didn't work, though – nah nah ne nah nah.

A: Banned me from watching TV for a month and made me eat vegetables. Yeuch!

H: Sent me much less money for my birthday than Rude Ralph's grandma sent him. It's not fair.

AT-AUNT GRETA

RICH AUNT RUBY

G VERA

PIMPLY PAUL

PRISSY POLLY

and

eve.

Make-Your-Own Models

Bring Horrid Henry and some of his enemies to life by making your own cardboard cut-out characters.

You will need:

Cardboard
Tracing Paper
Scissors
Pencils, pens or paints

Instructions:

1. Trace or copy a character onto your cardboard.
2. Colour it in.
3. Carefully cut it out along the dotted line, as shown on the template.
4. Make a base for your character by tracing or copying the base template onto your cardboard and cutting it out. Cut along the dotted line, and slot your character onto the base.

SAME LENGTH

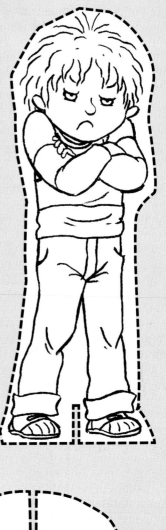

base

17

Who's Your Worst Enemy?

Do you have lots of evil enemies like Horrid Henry?
Find out which of Henry's enemies would be your worst.

1. Which of these sounds sets your teeth on edge?

(a)   Scratching and squeaking of a cello.

(b)   Tuneless tooting of a trumpet.

(c)   Fingernails scraping down a blackboard.

2. What would be the worst thing your enemy could do to you?

(a)   Take control of the TV.

(b)   Stay with you for a whole week.

(c)   Give you six hours of homework.

**3. How would you like to defeat
your enemy?**

(a) Sneak all the sweets from the tin
and let them take the blame.

(b) Empty a bucket of cold water
all over them.

(c) Flick paper pellets at their head when
they're not looking.

4. What sort of people make your blood boil?

(a)   Goody-goody, slimy sneaky toads.

(b)   Grumpy, grouchy show-offs.

(c)   Bossy, screechy know-it-alls.

5. What would be the perfect punishment for your enemy?

(a)   Exile them to an island with NO TV.

(b)   Let crocodiles loose in their bedroom.

(c)   Make them eat school dinners.

Answers

Mostly (a)s:

Your Number One Enemy is Horrid Henry's little brother, Perfect Peter. With his polite manners, tidy bedroom and goody-goody friends, he's the perfect enemy – especially if you're rude, untidy and horrid, like Henry!

Mostly (b)s:

Your top enemy is Henry's grouchy schoolmate and neighbour, Moody Margaret. It's not just that she's bad-tempered and bossy, but she also has the best clubhouse in the neighbourhood and all the latest toys – grrrr!

Mostly (c)s:

You must be very brave – your biggest enemy is scary Miss Battle-Axe! Forever giving loathsome lessons and dishing out horrible homework, you'll need to be cunning and courageous to battle with her.

Henry's Year

SO FAR...

Mum: So, how's your year so far?
Dad: ARRRRRGGHHHHH!

19

What's in the Swag Bag?

What's Henry running away with in his swag bag?
Follow the tangled strings and find out.

What would you hide in your swag bag?

Horrid Henry's Birthday

It's Horrid Henry's birthday, and he's up early to open his presents. Henry has asked his mum and dad for loads of money. But what do they buy him instead? Follow the time clues below and write the letters in the answer spaces below.

Where does the big hand go when it's . . .

1. Quarter past six?
2. Twenty to seven?
3. Ten to seven?
4. Twenty-five past six?
5. Quarter past six?

6. Five past six?
7. Six o'clock?
8. Twenty-five to seven?
9. Quarter to seven?
10. Quarter past six?

11. Six o'clock?
12. Twenty-five to seven?
13. Twenty past six?

14. Ten past six?
15. Half past six?
16. Quarter past six?
17. Quarter to seven?
18. Quarter past six?

ANSWER: _ _ _ _ _ _ , _ _ _ _ _ _
_ _ _ _ _ _ _

When do kangaroos celebrate their birthdays?

During leap year!

21

Marvellous Money-Making Schemes

When Horrid Henry doesn't get any money for his birthday, he has to think of some cunning schemes to make some cold hard cash himself. Here are some of his best ever plans.

'Horrid Henry and the Fangmangler' from **Horrid Henry's Nits.**

'Fangmanglers only come out at night,' whispered Henry. 'They slip into the shadows then sneak out and . . . BITE YOU!' he suddenly shrieked.

The Best Boys Club members gasped with fright.

'I'm not scared,' said Peter. 'And I've never heard of a Fangmangler.'

'That's because you're too young,' said Henry. 'Grown-ups don't tell you about them because they don't want to scare you.'

'I want to see it,' said Tidy Ted.

'Me too,' said Spotless Sam and Goody-Goody Gordon.

Peter hesitated for a moment.

'Is this a trick, Henry?'

'Of course not,' said Henry. 'And just for that I won't let you come.'

'Oh please, Henry,' said Peter.

Henry paused. 'All right,' he said. 'We'll meet in the back garden after dark. But it will cost you two pounds each.'

'Two pounds!' they squealed.

'Do you want to see a Fangmangler or don't you?'

Perfect Peter exchanged a look with his friends.

They all nodded.

'Good,' said Horrid Henry. 'See you at six o'clock. And don't forget to bring your money.'

Tee hee, chortled Henry silently. Eight pounds! He could get a Dungeon Drink kit and a Grisly Ghoul Grub box at this rate.

'Horrid Henry's Thank You Letter' from **Horrid Henry's Underpants.**

And then suddenly Horrid Henry had a wonderful, spectacular idea. Why had he never thought of this before? He would be rich, rich, rich. 'There goes money-bags Henry,' kids would whisper enviously, as he swaggered down the street, followed by Peter lugging a hundred videos for Henry to watch in his mansion on one of his twenty-eight giant TVs. Mum and Dad and Peter would be living in their hovel somewhere, and if they were very very nice to him Henry might let them watch one of his smaller TVs for fifteen minutes or so once a month.

Henry was going to start a business. A business guaranteed to make him rich.

'Step right up, step right up,' said Horrid Henry. He was wearing a sign saying: 'HENRY'S THANK YOU LETTERS: Personal letters written just for you.' A small crowd of children gathered round him.

'Moody Margaret's Makeover' from **Horrid Henry and the Abominable Snowman.**

Horrid Henry had actually seen Margaret being paid. And good money, too, just for smearing some coloured gunk onto people's faces and yanking their hair about.

Hmmmn.

Horrid Henry started to think. Maybe Margaret *did* have a little eensy-weensy teeny-tiny bit of a good idea. And, naturally anything she could do, Henry could do much, much better. Margaret obviously didn't know the first thing about makeovers, so why should she make all that money, thought Horrid Henry indignantly. He'd steal – no, *borrow* – her idea and do it better. Much much better. He'd make people look really fantastic.

Henry's Makeovers. Henry's Marvellous Makeovers. Henry's Miraculous Makeovers.
He'd be rich!

Turn over the page to see Henry's amazing advert . . .

Are you ugly?
Are you very very ugly?
Do you look like the creature from
the black lagoon? (Only worse?)
Then today is your lucky day!

HENRY'S MARVELLOUS MAKEOVERS.

Only £2 for an exciting new you!!!!!

Find out if Henry really does become rich in **'Moody Margaret's Makeover'** from **Horrid Henry and the Abominable Snowman.**

If you can think of a magnificent money-making scheme, write it down here so you don't forget it!

_____

_____

_____

_____

_____

Henry's Year
SO FAR...

Henry: I hope you're having a really rotten year.
Margaret: No, I'm not! My Magnificent Makeovers were amazingly successful – even though you tried to copy me with your pathetic Marvellous (Not) Makeovers.
Henry: I stole loads of your customers – they all wanted a makeover from me, not you. Nah nah ne nah nah.

Spot the Difference

Can you find six differences between these two pictures?

1.

2.

3.

4.

5.

6.

The Purple Hand Secret Code

Horrid Henry and Rude Ralph have discovered a new code for their club – the Morse Code, made up of dots and dashes. Best of all, Henry and Ralph can send each other messages in the dark using their torches, giving a quick flash for a dot and a long

A . -   J . - - -   S . . .

B - . . .   K - . -   T -

C - . - .   L . - . .   U . . -

D - . .   M - -   V . . . -

E .   N - .   W . - -

F . . - .   O - - -   X - . . -

G - - .   P . - - .   Y - . - -

H . . . .   Q - - . -   Z - - . .

I . .   R . - .

Can you read this message?

. . .   - - -   . . -   . - .
. . .   . . -   -   . - -   -   - .
. .   . . .
. . .   -   . . -   - .   - . -   - - -

Henry: Sour Susan, how's your year so far?

Susan: I should have had a much better year, but because Margaret is such a big meanie and is always calling me Lazy Lump, and firing me from the Secret Club, and pretending she likes Linda and Gurinder more than me, I wasn't as happy as I should have been. I should be the leader of the Secret Club, not that moody old grouch Margaret. Why am I still friends with her????

Henry's Year SO FAR...

Top Trip Quiz

'School trips are boring,' moans Horrid Henry. 'Why can't we go somewhere fun?'
Try this quiz and see which would be your ideal school trip.

1. What do you like most about school trips?

(a)   Learning interesting new things about the world around us.

(b)   Getting away from lessons and going somewhere wet and muddy.

(c)   Having lots of fun and eating loads of sweets on the bus.

2. Who would you like to sit next to on the bus?

(a) The teacher or the parent helper.

(b) Uh . . . I dunno.

(c) Rude Ralph and Greedy Graham – at the back of the bus.

3. What would you like in your packed lunch?

(a) Egg and cress sandwiches on brown bread, carrot and celery sticks, and an apple.

(b) A large beef baguette and a monster chocolate bar.

(c) Crisps, biscuits, chocolate and a fizzywizz drink.

4. What would you pack in your bag to take with you?

(a) Pencil case and notepad – I don't want to miss out on any of the fascinating information.

(b) Wellies.

(c) Loads of money, chocolate and sweets.

5. When your teacher hands you a questionnaire to fill in, what do you do?

(a)   Answer every question in my best handwriting.

(b)   Oops! I've dropped it in a puddle.

(c)   Throw it straight in the nearest bin.

Answers

Mostly (a)s: Like Perfect Peter, you'd enjoy a trip to the Town Museum. You'd find the old relics fascinating, and would enjoy neatly completing your questionnaire and tucking into a healthy lunch.

Mostly (b)s: As you like getting your hands dirty, a trip to the countryside would suit you best. Like Beefy Bert, you'd enjoy the simple pleasures of fresh air, mud and getting to grips with the slimy pond life.

Mostly (c)s: Admit it, you don't want to go on a school trip at all – you want a day of fun-filled excitement with your friends. Just like Horrid Henry, your idea of a good day out is getting a million miles away from Miss Battle-Axe, heading for the funfair and indulging in fast food and even faster rides!

Henry's Year SO FAR...

Henry: How's your year so far?
Peter: I'm being as good as gold this year. I've eaten all my fruit and vegetables, and all of my sandwiches with the crusts on.

Spring Picture Maze

Can you find your way through this Spring picture maze?
Follow the path by moving along the squares with a leaf, flower,
egg or chick on them. You can only move one square at a time,
left, right, up or down, but not diagonally.

CLUE:
If you land on a square
with a wintry picture,
you've taken the
wrong path!

START

FINISH

Odd One Out

These six pictures of Moody Margaret with her Valentine's Day card from Horrid Henry look exactly the same, but one of them is different. Can you spot the odd one out?

Answer: _____

What's Your Style?

Take a look at what you're wearing and try this fun fashion quiz to find out if you share your sense of style with your favourite characters.

1. How would you describe your choice of clothes?

(a) Just anything picked up from the pile on my bedroom floor.

(b) Sensible, neat, tidy and smart. Perfect.

(c) Bright, colourful, and fashionable.

2. Do you like plain or patterned clothes?

(a) Stripes are cool.

(b) Plain clothes, in brown and grey.

(c) Flowery patterns or big splashes of colour.

3. What would you buy to wear if you had lots of money?

(a) I wouldn't buy clothes! I'd buy loads of brilliant toys.

(b) One smart new outfit. I'd save the rest of the money.

(c) Lots of multi-coloured tops and trousers.

4. What's your favourite item of clothing?

(a) Root-A-Toot trainers or big boots.

(b) A comfy cardigan or sweatshirt.

(c) Colourful trousers or shirt.

5. What's your idea of a nightmare outfit?

(a) A tight, frilly pageboy or bridesmaid outfit.

(b) Scruffy jeans and ripped T-shirt.

(c) Dull, dreary trousers with a dull, dreary top.

Answers

Mostly (a)s:

You might be a bit scruffy, but you certainly have your own style and you don't care what other people think. Just like you, Horrid Henry and Moody Margaret are both individuals when it comes to their clothes. Henry doesn't care what he wears, though he loves his Root-A-Toot trainers. And with her short skirt and big boots combination, and her spiky hairstyle, Moody Margaret always stands out in a crowd.

Mostly (b)s:

You have to admit that fashion isn't very important in your life. All your clothes are plain and practical, and you don't like trying anything different. Like Perfect Peter, you enjoy looking smart – but if your brightest garment is your school sweatshirt, it's time to give your wardrobe a revamp. Pester your parents for some new gear before you start to share your sense of style with Miss Battle-Axe and her sad, saggy cardigans!

Mostly (c)s:

Like Gorgeous Gurinder and Brainy Brian, you like your clothes to be colourful and fashionable. You dress to be noticed – and love vibrant colours and eye-catching patterns. Just like Spring, your clothes are fresh and bright – and everyone smiles when they see you coming.

Henry's Year

SO FAR...

Henry: How's your year so far?
Peter: I'm being as good as gold this year. I haven't forgotten to bring my hankie to school once.
Henry: Mum's just bought me some new Root-a-Toot trainers and she hasn't bought you any. Ha ha!

April Fool's Day Pranks

April Fool's Day is one of my favourite days because I get to defeat loads of my enemies with my fantastic pranks. Here's how I do some of my best tricks.

❋ Before breakfast, I sneak into the kitchen, open up all the boxes of cereals and pull out the bags. I put all the bags back – but in the wrong boxes. Then I watch my mum pour Sweet Tweet into her bowl instead of her yucky muesli.

❋ I pretend to be kind and helpful at breakfast by putting the milk into a jug. Then I sneak in a few drops of red food colouring – and wait until Mum, Dad and Peter pour PINK milk all over their muesli. Ha ha!

❋ Stuffing some screwed-up tissues or cotton wool into the toes of Mum and Dad's shoes is one of my top tricks. When they try to get dressed in the morning, they can't decide if their feet have grown or their shoes have shrunk. April fools!

❋ When Mum's not watching, I put some of her gross lipstick on my fingers. I tell Peter that he's got a funny mark on his face and pretend to be nice and wipe it off for him. But really I wipe the lipstick all over his soppy face. Hurray for Henry!

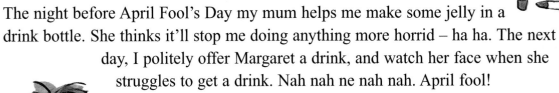

❋ The night before April Fool's Day my mum helps me make some jelly in a drink bottle. She thinks it'll stop me doing anything more horrid – ha ha. The next day, I politely offer Margaret a drink, and watch her face when she struggles to get a drink. Nah nah ne nah nah. April fool!

If you know a good April Fool's Day trick, send it to pranks@orionbooks.co.uk. You never know, Henry might try it!

Stinky Stinkbombs

Find out what Horrid Henry and Rude Ralph do with their stinkbomb in **Horrid Henry's Stinkbomb.**

Horrid Henry opened his Stinky Stinkbomb kit. He'd bought it with Grandma. Mum would never have let him buy it. But because Grandma had given him the money Mum couldn't do anything about it. Ha ha ha.

Now, which pong would he pick? He looked at the test tubes filled with powder and read the gruesome labels.

Bad breath. Dog poo. Rotten eggs. Smelly socks. Dead fish. Sewer stench.

'I'd go for dead fish,' said Ralph. 'That's the worst.'

Henry considered.

'How about we mix dead fish and rotten eggs?'

'Yeah,' said Rude Ralph.

HORRID HENRY'S SECRET STINKBOMB RECIPE

What I used:

A plastic container with a well-fitting lid

1 egg

Milk

Vinegar

A cocktail stick

How I made it:

1. I broke the egg into the plastic container and added a tablespoon of milk and a tablespoon of vinegar.
2. I put the lid on tight then hid the container somewhere warm.
3. After two days, I made 20 holes in the lid with the cocktail stick. Yeuch! What a stench!
4. I sneaked the stinkbomb into Peter's bedroom – and listened to his screams of horror!

Horrid Henry's Terrible Tricks

Then Henry had a wonderful, spectacular idea. This was it. The best plan he'd ever had. Someday someone would stick a plaque on the school wall celebrating Henry's genius. There would be songs written about him. He'd probably even get a medal.

As well as his April Fool's Day tricks and his stinky stinkbombs, Henry has planned all sorts of clever and complicated pranks. Which of these do you think is Henry's best idea?

Peter gave Henry his trainers, then lay still as a statue.

Horrid Henry grabbed the shoes, then dashed up the stairs to his classroom. It was empty. Good.

Horrid Henry went over to the window and opened it. Then he stood there, holding one of Peter's shoes in each hand.

Henry waited until he heard Mr Nerdon's footsteps. Then he went into action.

'Help!' shouted Horrid Henry. 'Help!'

Mr Nerdon entered. He saw Henry and glowered.

'What are you doing here? Get out!'

'Help!' shouted Henry. 'I can't hold on to him much longer . . . he's slipping . . . aahhh, he's fallen!'

Read the full story of Henry's perfect prank in **'Horrid Henry's New Teacher'**
in **Horrid Henry Tricks the Tooth Fairy.**

What if there was a way to get those sweets without the horrid hassle of learning to spell? Suddenly, Henry had a brilliant, spectacular idea. It was so simple Henry couldn't believe he'd never thought of it before.

He sat next to Clever Clare. Clare always knew the spelling words. All Henry had to do was to take a little peek at her work. If he positioned his chair right, he'd easily be able to see what she wrote. And he wouldn't be copying her, no way. Just double-checking. I am a genius, thought Horrid Henry. 100% right on the test. Loads of Big Bopper sweets. Mum and Dad would be so thrilled they'd let him watch extra TV. Hurray!

Find out if Henry gets the reward he wants in **'Horrid Henry's Homework'**
in **Horrid Henry and the Mummy's Curse.**

And then suddenly Horrid Henry had a brilliant, spectacular idea. Why had he never thought of it before? He'd ask to hoover every week.

Henry dragged the hoover over to the sitting room door and left it roaring there. Then he flopped on the sofa and switched on the TV. Great, Hog House hadn't finished!

VROOM, VROOM, VROOM.

Mum and Dad listened to the hoover blaring from the sitting room. Goodness, Henry was working hard. They were amazed.

Find out if Henry's hoover trick backfires in **'Horrid Henry's Chores'** in **Horrid Henry Meets the Queen.**

Rats. Despite his best efforts, it looked like Mum and Dad were going to carry on. Well, if he couldn't make them turn back, maybe he could delay them? Somehow? Suddenly Henry had a wonderful, spectacular idea. It couldn't be easier, and it was guaranteed to work. He'd miss the christening!

Mum, Dad and Peter got back in the car. Mum drove off.

'I need a wee,' said Henry.

'Not now, Henry.'

'I NEED A WEE!' screamed Henry. 'NOW!'

Mum headed back to the services.

Dad and Henry went to the toilets.

'I'll wait for you outside,' said Dad. 'Hurry up or we'll be late.'

Late! What a lovely word.

Henry went into the toilet and locked the door. Then he waited. And waited. And waited.

Finally, he heard Dad's grumpy voice.

'Henry? Have you fallen in?'

Henry rattled the door.

'I'm locked in,' said Henry. 'The door's stuck. I can't get out.'

Does Henry's delaying tactic work? Find out in **'Horrid Henry's Car Journey'** in **Horrid Henry and the Bogey Babysitter.**

Brainy Brian's Fascinating

Brainy Brian is a factoid fanatic and he knows all sorts of fantastic facts and figures. Try this quiz and find out if you have as many facts at your fingertips as Brainy Brian.

1. **Are there more bones in your hands or in your feet?**
   (a) Hands.
   (b) Feet.
   (c) The same number.

2. **How far could a fully-grown elephant jump?**
   (a) 0 metres.
   (b) 1 metre.
   (c) 2 metres.

3. **Which takes more muscle power – smiling or frowning?**
   (a) Smiling.
   (b) Frowning.
   (c) Both the same.

4. **How much weight can an ant lift?**
   (a) Its own bodyweight.
   (b) 10 times its own bodyweight.
   (c) 50 times its own bodyweight.

5. **What's the highest number of times you can fold a piece of paper?**
   (a) 5.
   (b) 7.
   (c) It depends on the size of the paper.

6. **What's the longest lifespan of a pet goldfish?**
   (a) 5 years.
   (b) 10 years.
   (c) 25 years.

7. **Is it possible to sneeze with your eyes open?**
   (a) Yes.
   (b) No.
   (c) Sometimes.

8. **How much time do ants spend asleep?**
   (a) 20 hours a day.
   (b) 8 hours a night.
   (c) None.

actoids

9. **Which creature lays the largest eggs in the world?**

(a) Ostrich.

(b) Shark.

(c) Eagle.

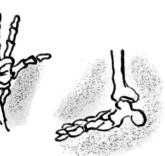

10. **Who have more bones, adults or children?**

(a) Adults.

(b) Children.

(c) Both the same.

11. **How heavy is a blue whale's tongue? As heavy as . . .**

(a) A cabbage.

(b) A cow.

(c) An elephant.

12. **What's the world record for hiccupping?**

(a) 26 years.

(b) 45 years.

(c) 68 years.

HIC!

Did you know? Our eyes always stay the same size, but our nose and ears never stop growing. If you don't believe me, just look at Miss Battle-Axe!

Henry's Year

SO FAR...

Henry: How's your year so far?
Peter: I'm being as good as gold this year. I'm never late to school and I always remember to bring my homework.

Sporting Stars

Horrid Henry's favourite activity is watching TV and eating crisps but even he likes to join in and play games. See which sports he and his classmates like best, and why.

Aerobic Al loves running because he likes going fast and keeping fit.

He's also keen on swimming because he's streamlined and speedy.

Horrid Henry likes the excitement of skateboarding and learning new tricks.

Kung-Fu Kate enjoys training to be a black belt in karate because it scares Horrid Henry!

The egg and spoon race is Perfect Peter's favourite at Sports' day because he has to be careful and keep his balance.

On Sports' day, Henry volunteers for the sack race so he can crash into people and knock them flying.

The girls like skipping games because even Moody Margaret and Sour Susan start smiling.

40

Moody Margaret loves football because she's the best footballer in the class.

Horrid Henry loves football because he's brilliant at shirt pulling and superb at screaming 'Offside!' and howling 'Come on, ref!'. He's great at toe-treading, elbowing, barging, pushing, shoving, tripping and . . . he once scored a GOAL!

Do you share a favourite sport with one of Horrid Henry's classmates? What is it and why do you like it?

_____

_____

_____

_____

_____

Henry's Year
SO FAR...

Henry: Hope you're having a stinky year.
Margaret: No way! I'm the best footballer in school and captain of the team. I only lost to Al's team because of your outrageous cheating.

41

Greedy Graham's Grub

Greedy Graham likes his grub, and ice-cream is one of his favourite treats. Try his delicious idea for an extra-special ice-cream extravaganza.

CHUNKY CHOCOLATE SENSATION

If you like all things chocolatey, then you'll love this rich ice-cream dream.

You will need:

Ice-cream, vanilla or chocolate, or both
Chocolate sauce
Your favourite chocolate bar or a chocolate chip cookie
Hundreds and thousands

Instructions:

1. Put one or two scoops of ice-cream in a dish.
2. Squirt on some chocolate sauce.
3. Roughly chop your favourite chocolate bar, or break up a chocolate chip cookie and scatter the pieces over the ice-cream.
4. Sprinkle with hundreds and thousands for a splash of colour.

Mmmm. Chocolate heaven!

Henry's Year SO FAR...

Henry: OK Bert, apart from knowing me, and having me in your class, and sharing a desk with me when Mr Nerdon was teaching us, and acting with me in the school play, and trying to copy my answers, what's been the highlight of your year?
Bert: I dunno.

Ice-cream Criss-cross

There are loads of yummy ingredients you can eat with ice-cream.
Can you fit the words below into the criss-cross puzzle?

4 LETTERS
NUTS

5 LETTERS
WAFER
FLAKE

6 LETTERS
BANANA

8 LETTERS
CHERRIES
ICECREAM
MERINGUE

9 LETTERS
CHOCOLATE

12 LETTERS
STRAWBERRIES
MARSHMALLOWS

CLUE: start with the two longest words

Why did Lazy Linda give cough medicine to her pony?

Because someone told her it was a little horse.

Happy Holidays

Horrid Henry's family holidays are a disaster. Henry's idea of a good holiday just isn't the same as his mum and dad's. What sort of holiday would suit you? Imagine your dream holiday, and answer these questions.

1. What do you dream of doing on holiday?
(a) Going for good long walks in the countryside – whatever the weather.
(b) Swimming in the sea, building sandcastles and enjoying the sunshine.
(c) Sitting on the sofa, eating crisps and watching TV.

2. What would be your perfect meal?
(a) Sausages and baked beans cooked over an open fire.
(b) A beach barbecue and a big ice-cream.
(c) Pizza, chips, burgers, crisps, chocolate and sweets.

3. What would you be wearing on your dream holiday?
(a) Walking boots, thick socks, waterproof trousers, woolly jumper and an anorak.
(b) Swimming trunks or a bikini.
(c) Pyjamas – it's a holiday!

4. What would you bring back with you?
(a) Muddy boots and soggy wet clothes.
(b) A collection of pebbles and shells.
(c) A collection of sweet wrappers and crisp packets.

5. What are your top three tips for a dream holiday?
(a) Fresh air, cold showers and quiet.
(b) Sun, sea and sand.
(c) Comfy beds, hot baths and a giant TV with fifty-seven channels.

What's round and green and goes camping?

A boy sprout.

Answers

Mostly (a)s: Unlike Henry, you like a challenge, and your ideal holiday is a camping trip without any home comforts. But would you enjoy sitting in a soggy tent with the rain drip-drip-dripping overhead? And how would you feel if you had to share your tent with some friendly visitors – like the cows from the next-door field?

Mostly (b)s: A traditional seaside holiday is your idea of bliss. So pack up your swimming gear, and your bucket and spade, and enjoy a fun-filled beach break.

Mostly (c)s: Just like Horrid Henry, your idea of a perfect holiday would be to spend every day grossing out on pizza, chips, crisps and sweets and watching all your favourite TV programmes. So why go on holiday when everything you need is at home?

Henry's Year

SO FAR...

Mum:
So, how's your year so far?
Dad:
ARRRRRGGHHHHH!

Crazy Car Games

Being on holiday with my stinky family is bad enough, but getting there stuck in a car next to the Duke of Poop is horrible.

If you need something to do when you're travelling, try out one of these games.

HORRID HENRY'S GAME

Henry is Horrid, Peter is Perfect and Margaret is Moody, but what about you and your family and friends? Whatever their names are, see if you can find some funny descriptive words that start with the same letter as their name. If you run out of people, you could use types of animals instead, for example: Daft Dog and Cunning Cat.

COUNTING CARS

Each person in the car has to spot 20 cars in a colour of their choice. The first person to spot all 20 is the winner. You can count other things you might see along the road too, like animals, or road signs, or people walking their dogs.

ALPHABET ANIMALS

Take it in turns to think of an animal beginning with each letter of the alphabet. The first person might say 'anteater' and the next person might say 'bear'.

Horrid Henry's sneaky cheat: If there are just two of you playing, make sure you go first, then your smelly little brother or sister will have to think of an animal beginning with 'X'. Ha ha!

Perfect Peter's Pencil and Paper Page

Some of Henry's car games are very noisy. To please your parents, why not try one of these pen and paper games?

Dotty Boxes

1. Draw a grid of dots. You can make this any size, but 8 dots by 8 dots is a good size to start with.

2. Take it in turns to draw a line between two dots, horizontally or vertically.

3. If your line makes one or more boxes, write your initials in them and take another turn.

4. The game is finished when all the dots are connected. The winner is the person who has completed the highest number of boxes.

Purple Hand Club Quiz

How much do you know about Horrid Henry's club, the Purple Hand? Take a look at the adventures Henry and his friends have, and try the questions to see if you're a member of the Clever or the Clueless Club.

'NUNGA!!!' screeched Henry again. 'You have to let me in! I know the password.'

'What do we do?' hissed Susan. 'You said anyone who knows the password enters.'

'For the last time, NUNGAAAAA!' shouted Horrid Henry.

'Nunga Nu,' said Margaret. 'Enter.'

Henry swaggered into the tent. Margaret glared at him.

Read **Horrid Henry and the Secret Club**

---

1. What happens next?

(a) Henry pretends to abandon the Purple Hand Club and joins the Secret Club instead.

(b) Henry stuffs his face with the Secret Club's special store of chocolate biscuits.

(c) Margaret and Susan tie Henry to a crate and leave him there so that he misses his lunch.

The sentry entered and gave the secret handshake.

'Henry, why—' began Perfect Peter.

'Call me by my title, Worm!'

'Sorry, Henry – I mean Lord High Excellent Majesty of the Purple Hand.'

'That's better,' said Henry. He waved his hand and pointed at the ground. 'Be seated, Worm.'

'Why am I Worm and you're Lord High Excellent Majesty?'

'Because I'm the Leader,' said Henry.

'I want a better title,' said Peter.

Find out what happens next in **Horrid Henry and the Bogey Babysitter**

---

2. What happens next?

(a) Henry allows Peter to be called Lord Worm.

(b) Henry tells Peter to go away and says he can't be in the Purple Hand any more.

(c) Peter runs off to tell their mum that Henry is calling him names.

Horrid Henry rubbed his hands. This was fantastic! At last, he had a spy in the enemy's camp! He'd easily defend himself against that stupid stinkbomb. Margaret would only let it off when he was in the fort. His sentry would be on the lookout armed with a goo-shooter. When Margaret tried to sneak in with her stinkbomb – ker-pow!

'Hang on a sec,' said Horrid Henry. 'Why should I trust you?'

The traitor is uncovered in **Horrid Henry's Stinkbomb**

3. Who is the traitor?

(a) Perfect Peter.

(b) Lazy Linda.

(c) Sour Susan.

'Whose club is this?' said Henry fiercely.

Peter's lip began to tremble.

'Yours,' muttered Peter.

'So if you want to stay as a temporary member, you have to do as I say,' said Henry.

'OK,' said Peter.

'And remember, one day, if you're very good, you'll be promoted from junior sentry to chief sentry,' said Henry.

'Ooh,' said Peter, brightening.

Business settled, Horrid Henry reached for the biscuit tin. He'd saved five yummy chocolate fudge chewies for today.

All is revealed in **Horrid Henry and the Bogey Babysitter**

4. What happens next?

(a) Henry eats all the biscuits and doesn't share any of them with Peter.

(b) Henry discovers that the biscuit tin is empty.

(c) When Henry opens the tin, Peter grabs the biscuits and runs home.

Go to the back of the book for the answers. If you got them all right – CONGRATULATIONS! You deserve to be a member of the Purple Hand Club. If you got any of them wrong, read the stories in *Horrid Henry and the Secret Club, Horrid Henry and the Bogey Babysitter* and *Horrid Henry's Stinkbomb*.

Find the Flags . . .

Horrid Henry's Purple Hand Club have sneaked into
Moody Margaret's garden and hidden eight of their flags.
But where are they?

Write down where the flags are hidden:

1 _____ 2 _____

3 _____ 4 _____

5 _____ 6 _____

7 _____ 8 _____

. . . and Hunt the Hats

Moody Margaret's Secret Club have taken their revenge and hidden eight of their pirate hats in Horrid Henry's garden. Can you find these too?

Write down where the hats are hidden:

1 _____ 2 _____

3 _____ 4 _____

5 _____ 6 _____

7 _____ 8 _____

Find the Perfect Pairs

Perfect Peter is Henry's Enemy Number One.
Can you find the four matching pairs?

A.

B.

C.

D.

E.

F.

G.

H.

The four matching pairs are:

___ and ___

___ and ___

___ and ___

___ and ___

52

Club Crossword

Test your club knowledge and see if you can complete Henry's crossword, by answering the questions below.

ACROSS

1. No one from the BEST _ _ _ _ CLUB is in the picture.
3. What are the Purple Hand biscuits kept in?
7. Who is sitting on the bucket?
8. Who is wearing a red top?
10. What colour is Moody Margaret's skirt?

DOWN

2. Horrid Henry's stripy top is BLUE and _ _ _ _ _ _ ?
4. What's the first word of the Secret Club's password?
5. Margaret's stripy top is white and - - - - - - ?
6. What is Sour Susan wearing?
9. Who is the Leader of the Purple Hand Club?
11. What's the last word of the Secret Club's password?

Henry's Year SO FAR...

Henry: The Purple Hand Club is best this year – and every year.
Margaret: Huh! Aren't you forgetting that the Secret Club destroyed your stupid club by spiking your fizzywizz drinks with a special secret potion from my Dungeon Drinks kit?

53

Rude Ralph's Revolting Volcano

Rude Ralph likes making lots of mess. Here's how he made a smelly volcanic explosion using ingredients from his kitchen.

For the mountain he used:

6 cups of flour
2 cups of salt
4 tablespoons of cooking oil
2 cups of water
An empty plastic bottle – the smaller the better
A baking tray
Lots of newspaper

How Ralph did it:

1. In a large bowl, Ralph mixed the flour, salt, oil and water together. He started by using a fork or spoon, then used his hands to knead the mixture into a stiff dough.
2. He covered the table with newspaper, and put the empty bottle on the baking tray.
3. Ralph modelled the dough around the bottle and moulded it into a mountain shape.
4. He made sure he didn't cover the top of the bottle or drop any dough into it.

For the explosion he used:

Warm water
Bicarbonate of soda
1/4 cup vinegar
Red food colouring
Washing-up liquid
A small jug

How Ralph did it:

1. Ralph put two tablespoons of bicarbonate of soda into the jug and carefully poured it into the plastic bottle.
2. He put a quarter of a cupful of warm water into the jug, added a teaspoonful of red food colouring and poured this into his plastic bottle.
3. Then he squirted in six drops of washing-up liquid.
4. Finally he put quarter of a cupful of vinegar into his jug, slowly poured it into the plastic bottle – and enjoyed the explosion.

Horrid Henry's Best Little Brother-Taming Tips

- Take charge of the TV remote control and tell your little brother that you are banning Daffy and her Dancing Daisies, Manners with Maggie and Nellie's Nursery for his own good.

- Surprise your little brother by letting him join your club. He'll be so grateful that he won't mind keeping guard all day.

- Let your little brother give you a cuddle – but only when you've got nits.

- If your little brother wants to look like you, encourage him. The more identical you and your little brother look, the better. Parents are easily confused, and you can make sure he gets the blame for something you did.

- If you're short of cash, you could always set up a stall and sell your little brother. Tell him he'll be going to a good home.

- Don't let your little brother beat you at anything or he'll get too big for his boots. Cheating usually works.

- Never let him forget that you're the oldest, the biggest and the cleverest.

Henry

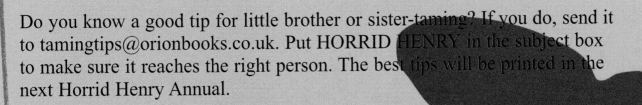

Do you know a good tip for little brother or sister-taming? If you do, send it to tamingtips@orionbooks.co.uk. Put HORRID HENRY in the subject box to make sure it reaches the right person. The best tips will be printed in the next Horrid Henry Annual.

Spooky Sleepover

Horrid Henry is having a spooky sleepover. His friends are coming in fancy dress, and he's planning some scary games.

Pass the Ghost

Henry's ghostly version of pass the parcel.

• Sneak into your little brother's bedroom, pinch one of his clean, white socks and stuff it with sweets. Fasten the end with a rubber band, and draw on a ghostly face with a black felt-tip pen.

• Sit everyone in a circle, put on some brilliant music like Killer Boy Rats and pass around the sock.

• When the music stops, the person holding the sock is out of the game.

• When there's only one person left, they win the sock and all the sweets.

If your little brother wins, tell him he's won his sock, and has to share the sweets. That's the rules. Ha ha!

Mummy Race

The object of this game is to wrap your partner in toilet paper as fast as possible.

• Grab all the toilet paper from the bathroom when your mum's not looking.
• Put everybody into pairs. One person has to do the wrapping and the other person has to be mummified alive.

The team with the first person to be completely covered is the winner.

Pin on the Nose

A monstrous version of pin the tail on the donkey.

- On a big piece of paper or cardboard, draw the scariest creature you can think of – a witch or a monster or, even scarier, Miss Battle-Axe. Draw in their eyes and mouth, but put a large X where the nose should be.
- On separate pieces of paper, draw as many noses as you will need, and put some sticky tape or fixers on the back of each one.
- Blindfold each person in turn and give them a nose.
- Spin the first person around a few times. Stop them when they're facing the picture. They have to try and stick the nose in the right place.
- When everyone's had a go, the person with the nose closest to the X is the winner.

Murder in the Dark

A brilliant game for scaring big babies like Perfect Peter.

- Make enough slips of paper for all your guests. On one of them write 'murderer', on another write 'detective' and on all the rest write 'suspect'. Fold them up to hide the writing.
- Put the slips in a bowl, and let everyone pick one. Don't tell anybody else what you are, unless you are the detective.
- If you are the detective, go and wait outside the room, turning off the light as you go.
- Now the fun starts. In the dark, the murderer chooses a victim and taps that person on the shoulder. The victim falls to the ground.
- When someone stumbles over the 'body', he shouts, 'Murder in the Dark'.
- The detective returns to the scene of the crime, turns the light back on – and tries to guess who committed the murder.

Scary Dot-to-dot

Join the dots, and find out why Rude Ralph, Anxious Andrew, Gorgeous Gurinder, Beefy Bert and Moody Margaret look so scared.

How do you spot a modern spider?

He doesn't have a web — he has a website!

Clever Clare's Wormery

Clever Clare likes exploring all kinds of nature, especially creepy-crawlies. Here's how she made a simple wormery to watch what worms get up to under the soil.

You will need:

A large glass or plastic jar – the giant jars of chocolates
from Christmas are ideal
Soil
Sand
Black paper or a dark-coloured cloth
Leaves or grass
3 or 4 worms

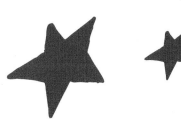

How to do it:

1. Fill the jar with five layers of soil and sand.
    Start and end with a layer of soil.

2. Water the soil so that it's damp, but not soaking.
    Remember to water your wormery every three days.

3. Find three or four worms in your garden, and put them
    in your wormery.

4. Cover the top with leaves or grass for the worms to eat.

5. Cover the wormery with the black paper or cloth, and
    leave in a cool place.

6. In a few days' time, have a look. You'll see
    tunnels through the layers, and the worms will have
    pulled the food down into the soil. Give your worms
    some more food, wrap up your
    wormery again, and leave for a few more days.

7. Next time you look, you might find
    that the worms have completely mixed
    up the layers of soil and sand.

8. Empty your wormery back into
    the garden, and set your
    worms free.

Why don't baby birds smile?

Would you like it if your mother fed you worms all day?

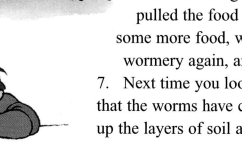

59

Magic Martha's Magic Trick

Magic Martha likes entertaining her friends and family with her magic tricks. Here's her clever coin trick, which is easy to master.

You will need:
Five coins – all different if possible

How to do it:

1. Lay out the coins in front of you on a table or on the floor. Make sure that they are all facing heads up, but try not to let your audience see that this is what you're doing. Act casual.

2. Choose a volunteer from the audience who won't run off with your money. Tell your audience that you're going to turn round so that you can't see what's happening.

3. Ask your volunteer to turn over any two coins at the same time. They can do this a number of times if they wish. The important thing is that they always turn over TWO AT A TIME.

4. Ask your volunteer to slide any one of the coins forward and cover it with their hand.

5. Turn round and tell your audience that you are able to see through your volunteer's hand and will be able to tell them whether the coin is heads up or tails up.

6. While you are chatting to your audience, sneak a peek at the other four coins. Count how many are heads up. If it's an even number, then the coin under your volunteer's hand is heads up. If it's an odd number, then the coin under your volunteer's hand is tails up.

7. Tell your audience whether it's heads or tails, and ask your volunteer to reveal the coin. Hey presto!

Horrid Henry's Guide to Good Manners

🌟 When you receive an unwanted present . . .
Shout AARRGGHH! Bleech! Ick! Yuck! Sling it on the floor and stomp on it. Always write an honest thank you letter and say what a horrible, useless present it was. Lying is extremely bad manners.

🌟 When you're asked to share . . .
If someone has something you want, like the remote control, tell them it's rude to share. Pounce on them, grab the remote, and push them to the floor.

🌟 When you need your mum . . .
Why go all the way downstairs to talk to your mum? If you scream 'MUM!' from your bedroom, she can hear you anyway.

🌟 When your mum and dad have guests for dinner . . .
Use your Grisly Grub box to make some Nasty Nuts and Rotten Crispies. Put on your sweetest smile and serve these tasty snacks to the guests. Your parents will thank you when their guests leave early.

🌟 When meeting the Queen . . .
Don't just say 'hi'. The Queen likes a lot of attention. You have to curtsey, put your thumb on your nose and wriggle your fingers. And ask her lots of interesting questions, like how many TVs she has at the palace.

🌟 When friends come to stay . . .
Guests always come last. Don't let them play with your toys, or sit on your chair or sleep in your bed, or they might never want to leave. Make sure they don't feel sad when it's time to go home.

🌟 When eating . . .
Always eat with your fingers. A knife and fork slows you down too much, and it's rude to keep others waiting.

Henry

Brainy Brian's Big Quiz

It's time to try Brainy Brian's ten horrible headscratchers and test your in-depth knowledge of Horrid Henry. Are you leaping ahead in the league tables or have you been left behind?

1. What sort of snowman does Moody Margaret make for the Frosty Freeze Ice-Cream Best Snowman Competition?
(a) A pirate.
(b) A ballerina.
(c) A rabbit.

2. What's the name of Perfect Peter's teacher?
(a) Miss Lovely.
(b) Miss Sweet.
(c) Miss Jolly.

3. One of Perfect Peter's favourite programmes is called . . . ?
(a) Daisy and her Dancing Daffodils.
(b) Dandelion and her Dabbling Ducks.
(c) Daffy and her Dancing Daisies.

4. Which of these do you think would be the worst punishment for Horrid Henry?
(a) No TV for a week.
(b) No school for a week.
(c) No apples for a week.

5. Horrid Henry has a baby cousin called Vera. What's her nickname?
(a) Vicious Vera.
(b) Vomiting Vera.
(c) Vain Vera.

6. What kind of instrument does Moody Margaret play?
(a) Trumpet.
(b) Trombone.
(c) Tuba.

7. When Horrid Henry and Perfect Peter need a babysitter, they get the toughest teen in town? Is it . . . ?
(a) Angry Anna.
(b) Rabid Rebecca.
(c) Crabby Chris.

8. Which part does Horrid Henry play in the school Christmas nativity?
(a) Blade of grass.
(b) Back legs of the donkey.
(c) Innkeeper.

. Which is Horrid Henry's favourite restaurant?
a) The Virtuous Veggie.
b) Gobble and Go.
c) Restaurant Le Posh.

**0. When Henry writes his will, what does
e leave to Perfect Peter?**
a) His sweet wrappers and a muddy twig.
b) His Goo-Shooter.
c) His lime green cardigan.

**urn to page 74 to see how many answers you got right and see how
much of a Horrid Henry expert you are!**

-10
Vell done! You're a real Horrid Henry whizz-kid. Carry on reading the books and
eep up the good work.

-6
Good, but you could do even better. Pester your parents for all the Horrid Henry
ooks, and aim to achieve an even higher mark.

-3
Jh-oh! Everything you know about Horrid Henry would fit on the back of a postage stamp.
t's time for some serious swotting.

Purple Hand Christmas Cards

Horrid Henry has a brilliant money-making scheme for Christmas. He's going to make lots of Christmas cards and wrapping paper decorated with his special Purple Hand prints to sell to his family and friends.

You will need:

Pieces of A4 cardboard or thick paper for the cards
A roll of brown packing paper for the wrapping paper
Poster paints
Felt-tip pens

How to do it:

1. If you're making Christmas cards, fold your pieces of card in half.

FOLD

2. Squirt out a good dollop of purple poster paint onto a plate or palette. If you don't have any purple paint, mix together red and blue to get the right shade.

3. Press your hand into the paint, then make a handprint on the front of the card.

4. Leave to dry.

5. If you're making wrapping paper, roll out the brown paper onto the table, and make your purple handprints all over the paper.

Horrid Henry's Rotten Rhymes

My name is Horrid Henry
I hate fresh air
I like to lounge around
On the comfy black chair

TO THE MOODIEST MARGARET
Margaret, you old pants face
I've never seen such a nutcase
You are a stinky smelly toad
Won't I laugh when you explode

Dear Old baldy Dad
Don't be sad
Be glad
Because you've had...
A very merry Christmas
Love from your Lad,
Henry

Dear Old wrinkly Mum
Don't be glum
Cause you've got a fat tum
And an even bigger brum
Love from your son,
Henry

Henry's Year
SO FAR...

Dad:
So, how's your year
so far?

Mum:
ARRRRRGGHHHHH!

Are you as good at writing poems as Horrid Henry?
Why not have a go – Horrid Henry thinks they make
great Christmas presents.

Christmas Sudoku

Can you fill in the coloured boxes so that each one contains a holly leaf, a Christmas stocking, a bauble and a present? Don't forget – every row across and column down must contain all four pictures too.

Try this one too.

How do snowmen get around?

They ride an icicle.

Henry's Year SO FAR...

Henry: For my best magic trick this year I made all the ice-cream disappear from the freezer.

66

. . . Nah Nah Ne Nah Nah!

Peter: I'm being as good as gold this year. But my brother Henry keeps calling me horrible names like Nappy Face, Worm and Wibble Pants.

Ralph: Yah, boo, sucks. Pllllllllluuugghh. Okay everyone, why did Peter take toilet paper to the party? Because he's a party pooper!!!

Henry: Lazy Linda, how's your year so far?
Linda: Yawn. I wish I had had more sleep this year. I've asked for a new pillow for Christmas, but I don't know if I will get out of bed on Christmas day to see what presents I got, I might be too tired – yawn.

Peter: I'm being as good as gold this year. I'm the tidy monitor at school, along with my friends Tidy Ted and Goody-Goody Gordon.

Henry: C'mon, Bert, don't be shy. All right, what disasters happened to you this year? The time you couldn't spell 'cat'? Or when you couldn't remember what presents to ask Father Christmas for? Or how about the time you couldn't remember if you were a sheep or a blade of grass in the nativity play I starred in?
Bert: Uhhh . . . I dunno.

Mum:
So, how was your year so far?
Dad:
ARRRRRGGHHHHH!

Moody Margaret's Year

It's been a fantastic year for me and my Secret Club members. Thanks to my clever plotting, we destroyed Henry's Purple Hand Club by spiking their fizzywizz drinks with a special secret potion from my Dungeon Drinks kit. It was so funny when Henry and Ralph started screaming and shrieking after I'd tricked them. Plus I managed to get Peter to become my spy, which meant I was able to foil Henry's plot to spike OUR Dungeon Drinks. Then I stole his pirat flag and forced him to give me mine back. And of course Susan and I managed to steal Henry's entire fort right from under his smelly nose. And then the great trick I played on Henry by pretending that he had hypnotised me and then spilling chocolate mousse and a fizzywizz drink all over him. Nah nah ne nah nah!

As I am the best actor in the class (and the world) I was naturally chosen to be Mary i the Nativity Play. I had more lines than anyone, and my mum and dad said that I was so fantastic that they hadn't even noticed there was anyone else on stage.

I am officially the Makeover Queen, with my terrific money-making success, Margaret's Magnificent Makeovers Henry is such a copy-cat he tried to copy me with his pathetic, so-called Henry's Marvellous (Not) Makeovers, but failed miserably as he made a complete mess of Soraya and Kate. Boy, were they sorry

they let him make them over. And of course, as captain and the best footballer in school, I led my team to many victories. I only lost to Al's team because of Henry's total and outrageous cheating. All I can say is, 'Margaret rules! Three cheers for Margaret!!!'

Perfect Peter's Year

have had a lovely year, thank you for asking. I was in the Good
s Gold Book eight times, five times more than anyone in our
chool's history. Miss Lovely gave me a perfect report. Mum and
Dad were so pleased with me, they kept asking Henry why he couldn't get good reports
ke me. I was a tidy monitor again for the second time in a row, along with my friends
idy Ted and Goody-Goody Gordon.

I ate all of my fruit and vegetables, ate all of my
sandwiches with the crusts on, and I never forgot to
bring a hankie to school. Plus I was never late and
always remembered to bring my homework.

You won't be surprised to hear that I played
Joseph in the school Nativity Play. Henry tried to
ruin my performance but I am too good an actor to
be distracted by anyone being horrid. Miss Lovely
said I was the
best person in
the entire play, but everyone
is important, even the blades of grass and the
winkling stars.

I was also chosen to give flowers to the Queen when
he came to our school. The Queen said, 'How lovely,'
when I gave her the bouquet. I got a little confused
about whether I should bow or curtsey, but I don't think
nyone noticed.

My wonderful snowbunny beat Henry's ugly
Abominable Snowman and Margaret's ballerina

snowgirl and every other snowman on the street to win the Frosty Freeze Ice-Cream factory Best Snowman Competition. Unfortunately the prize was lots of ice-cream which I don't like. I asked if I could change my prize to a year's supply of my favourite vegetables, but sadly they said no. So if anyone wants some Chunky Chocolate Fab Fudge Caramel Delight, or Squishy Squashy fudgy Marshmallow toffee whip, there's loads at my house.

My favourite author, Milksop Miles, writer of the world's best book, *The Happy Nappy*, visited my school! We all got to sing along with him, act out the super story, and sing the Happy Nappy song. I played Gappy Nappy. Henry was supposed to be the Happy Nappy, but he got too scared. Which was strange because no one in the Infants was scared, just Henry.

I also started my first newspaper, The Best Boys' Busy Bee. It costs 5p and I sell it at my school every day if you want to buy a copy.

My brother Henry played a lot of mean tricks on me this year and keeps calling me Nappy Face, Worm, Poopsicle, Duke of Poop, Ugly, Toad, and Wibble Pants even though I have TOLD him and TOLD him not to. But I did get my revenge on him by writing a note to Margaret asking her to marry him and signing it, Henry. It was a great revenge – until Henry found out. Oh well.

My New Year's resolutions are to try to be even more perfect.

Horrid Henry's Year

Wow, what a brilliant, amazing spectacular year I've had! So many great triumphs. So many evil enemies beaten into the dust. Like the time Miss Battle-Axe made me go to Miss Lovely's class for

no reason at all and I almost missed my favourite author TJ Fizz reading from her new book, *Skeleton Skunk*, but I managed to escape just in time. Hurray for Henry! Or the time Mum said there was no way she would buy me Root-a-Toot trainers, and then, hey presto, those Root-a-

Toots were on my feet, bugle-blasting around my house! Or the time Mum and Dad wouldn't let me go trick or treating and I *still* got loads of sweets!

What about the brilliant way I raided the Secret Club biscuit tin five times, and never got caught? That's 'cause I made it look as if Susan and Linda had robbed the tin

(Ha ha, Margaret, you old pants face, I'm better than you, nah nah ne nah nah!). And I stole their flag. And their secret code book. And even their secret club tent! I also set a booby trap. It was wonderful hearing them all shrieking when they got drenched. And then I stinkbombed them! Plus I managed to get Susan to become my spy, which meant I was able to foil Margaret's plot to stinkbomb us.

As I am the best actor in the school (and the world) I starred in the school Nativity Play as the Innkeeper – I way improved my part, because for some reason I was only given one puny line. That day a star was born: it was as if there was no one else on stage. Plus I scored the best goal ever in the class football match. And I got my arch enemy Bossy Bill out of my school. I don't think he'll be bothering me again for a while . . .

Let's see, what other fantastic and spectacular things happened to me this year? Of course, there are all my new joke books (please buy loads and loads of copies of them, as all the money will go to a child in need – heh heh).

Plus, I launched my new business, Henry's Marvellous Makeovers, and had loads and loads and loads of happy customers. That copy-cat Margaret's so-called Magnificent Makeovers didn't stand a chance while Henry the Makeover King was around! I stole all her customers and Soraya and Kate were especially delighted with how fantastic they looked. Then of course I hypnotised Margaret and made her think she was a chicken – ha ha. And she had to call me master and bring me all her sweets.

Christmas was especially great. We got to have pizza for lunch, and pudding first – hurrah! And no sprouts! No peas! No carrots! Plus, Rich Aunt Ruby finally gave me a decent present: CASH! It's still not enough to make up for all the horrid lime green jumpers and boxes of stationery she's given me in the past, though, so I will remind her to double the amount next time in the thank you note that Mum will make me write . . .

Unfortunately, my wormy toad brother is still around. And even though his silly pimple of a snow lump won the snowman-building contest by complete accident and total unfairness as my abominable snowman was so great, I've been able to sneak into the kitchen and eat most of his ice-cream prize every week! And then blame Mum for the missing ice-cream. And Dad. And Fluffy. I've also played some spectacular tricks on my nappy-face smelly pants brother. He believed there were fairies at the bottom of our

garden (boy did he get into trouble when he got caught outside after midnight by Mum and Dad). He believed I'd invented a time machine and that we could travel into the future. And I have managed to sneak at least fourty-seven of his chips without his noticing, plus filled up his plate with my peas and spinach and broccoli.

Henry rules! Three cheers for Henry!!

Puzzle Answers

Page 11 –
Hunt the Gizmos

Page 15	Page 44
Page 20	Page 59
Page 28	Page 60
Page 36	Page 64
Page 39	Page 66

Page 14 –
Horrid Henry's Evil Enemies

Grandma	h
Mum	a
Rich Aunt Ruby	d
Stuck-up Steve	f
Pimply Paul	g
Dad	i
Great-Aunt Greta	j
Perfect Peter	e
Vomiting Vera	b
Prissy Polly	c

Page 20 –
What's in the Swag Bag
Henry has all Root-A-Toot
trainers in his swag bag.

Page 21 –
Horrid Henry's Birthday
SOCKS, PANTS AND VESTS

Page 26 – Spot the Differences
The six differences are:
1. The pleats are missing from
   Moody Margaret's skirt.
2. The pocket is missing from
   Beefy Bert's jacket.

3. Rude Ralph's trousers are
   yellow instead of white.
4. The lines on the window
   are missing.
5. Horrid Henry's trainers
   are red instead of green.
6. Weepy William's eyebrow
   is missing.

Page 27 –
The Purple Hand Secret Code
The Morse Code message says:
SOUR SUSAN IS STINKY

Page 30 – Spring Picture Maze

Page 31 – Odd One Out
F is the odd one out because
Moody Margaret's top has
red stripes.

Page 38 – Brainy Brian's
Fascinating Factoids
1. (a) Hands
There are 26 bones in each of
your feet, but your hands just beat
that with 27 bones in each.
2. (a) 0 metres
Elephants are the only animals
that cannot jump.
3. (b) Frowning
It takes 43 muscles to frown but
only 17 to smile.
4. (c) 50 times its own
bodyweight
5. (b) 7
Whatever the size or thickness of
the paper, it can't be folded more
than seven times. Try it and see.
6. (c) 25 years
7. (b) No
If you don't believe this, watch
someone sneeze.
8. (c) None
Ants don't sleep at all.
9. (b) Shark
10. (b) Children
Children have 300 bones, but
adults only have 206. As we grow
some of our bones join together.
11. (c) An elephant
Don't ever let a blue whale give
you a friendly lick.
12. (c) 68 years
The record for hiccupping is
held by a pig farmer in America.
He only spent 29 years of his life
not hiccupping.

Page 43 – Ice-cream Criss-cross

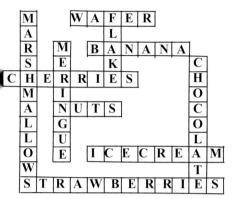

		W	A	F	E	R			
M			L						
A		M		B	A	N	A	N	A
R		E		K					C
S		R		I					H
C	H	E	R	R	I	E	S		O
M		I		N	U	T	S		C
A		N		G					O
L		G		U					L
L		U		E		I	C	E	C	R	E	A	M		A
O		E							T
W									
S	T	R	A	W	B	E	R	R	I	E	S

Page 48 – Purple Hand Club Quiz

1. b
2. a
3. c
4. b

Pages 50/51 – Find the Flags

Page 52 – Find the Perfect Pairs

The pairs are:

A and G

B and E

C and H

D and F

Page 53 – Club Crossword

¹B	O	²Y	S				³T	I	⁴N
		E			⁵P				U
⁶D		L		⁷S	U	S	A	N	
⁸R	A	L	P	⁹H	R				G
E		O		E	P				A
S		W		N	L				
S			¹⁰G	R	E	E	¹¹N		
				Y			U		

Page 58 – Scary Dot-to-Dot

Henry's friends are frightened of the spider.

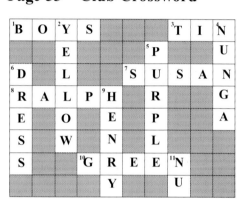

Page 62 – Brainy Brian's Big Quiz

1. b
2. a
3. c
4. a
5. b
6. a
7. b
8. c
9. b
10. a

Page 66 – Christmas Sudoku

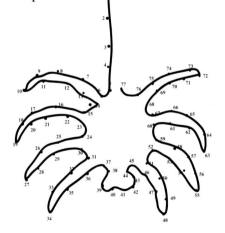

You can read these other *Horrid Henry* titles and all of them are available as audio editions, read by Miranda Richardson